W9-BRY-454

BUSTER'S BIG DAY

Based on the teleplay "Buster the Lost Dog" by Clark Stubbs

Illustrated by Lorraine O'Connell

A Random House PICTUREBACK® Book

Random House 🏠 New York

© 2014 Viacom International Inc. All rights reserved. Published in the United States by Random House Children's Books, a division of Random House, Inc., 1745 Broadway, New York, NY 10019, and in Canada by Random House of Canada Limited, Toronto. Originally published in different form as *Dog Days* in 2013. Pictureback, Random House, and the Random House colophon are registered trademarks of Random House, Inc. Nickelodeon, Team Umizoomi, and all related titles, logos, and characters are trademarks of Viacom International Inc. randomhouse.com/kids
ISBN 978-0-385-37520-7
MANUFACTURED IN CHINA
10 9 8 7 6 5 4 3 2

It was a sunny day at the Umi City Park. Team Umizoomi was playing with their friend Buster the dog.

"Buster wants to play fetch," Geo said. He threw the ball really far, and Buster chased after it.

How many balls
do you see?

Buster followed the bouncing ball into the back
of a truck. Suddenly, the truck drove away—with Buster!

"*Great Gigabytes!*" exclaimed Bot. "That truck is taking Buster to a construction site! We've got to save him. Team, it's time for action!"

How many shovels do you see?

Team Umizoomi jumped into UmiCar. "Let's go to the construction site," Milli said.

"We've got to save Buster!" cried Geo. UmiCar revved his engine, then took off through Umi City.

UmiCar jumped over a giant mud puddle.
"Go, UmiCar! Go!" Team Umizoomi cheered.

When UmiCar came to a bridge, he screeched to a halt. There was a red stop sign.

"The bridge is broken," announced DoorMouse. "Nobody can go across until somebody fixes it."

"What will we do?" Milli wondered. "We have to cross the bridge to get to the construction site."

"You fixed the bridge!" DoorMouse cheered as he changed the red sign to a green one.

"Now we can drive to the construction site and save Buster," said Milli. UmiCar quickly sped away.

At last, Team Umizoomi arrived at the construction site. They saw wheelbarrows and trucks and cranes, but they didn't see Buster. "I wonder where Buster could be," said Bot.

How many red things do you see?

"Look!" shouted Geo. "Buster is stuck in that red bucket! Don't worry, we'll get you down, boy!"

Team Umizoomi climbed to the top of the building, and Buster jumped to them. Then they all slid down a girder together.

"Now let's get back to the park," said Milli. Buster barked happily as the team climbed onto his back.

"Go, Buster!" everyone cheered.

Team Umizoomi rode Buster all the way back to the Umi City Park. "What an amazing day," Bot said. "I feel a celebration coming on!" *"Ruff! Ruff!"* Buster agreed, and everybody danced and shook happily.

Super Shapes!

2

8

10

Team Umizoomi had rescued Brownie! As everyone jumped out of the bucket, Bot shouted, "I feel a celebration coming on!" *"Meow!"* Brownie purred happily, and Team Umizoomi cheered and danced.

Milli and Geo climbed into the water bucket, and Bot lowered it into the well.

At the bottom of the well, Milli and Geo shouted, "Jump, Brownie! Jump!" The cat jumped into the bucket and gave Milli and Geo big thank-you licks. Then Bot raised the bucket.

The balloon landed near the well. Team
Umizoomi could hear Brownie meowing.
"She sounds really scared," Milli said.
"We're coming for you, Brownie!"

Team Umizoomi jumped into the hot-air balloon, and it carried them into the sky. They soared over the mountain.

How many orange stripes are on the balloon?

"We need a hot-air balloon to get over the mountain," said Geo. "I can build one with a circle, a triangle, and a square. *Super Shapes!*"

"*Great Gizmos!*" exclaimed Bot. "This is a mighty fine tractor!"
The engine rumbled as the tractor rolled over the green hills.
"We're coming for you, Brownie!" cried Milli. Team Umizoomi
chugged toward a big mountain.

How many
chickens can
you count?

"To cross the farm, we have to build a tractor," said Geo. "We need a square, a trapezoid, and two circles. *Super Shapes!*"

"Life vests on!" said Geo. "Now let's go rescue that cat!"
Team Umizoomi raced down the river to the farm.

"And if we split this rectangle, we can make the windshield," he added.

"To turn these shapes into a super speedboat, say *'Super Shapes!'*"

Team Umizoomi ran to the river. "I can make a speedboat with my Super Shapes Splitter!" said Geo. "If we cut this oval in half, we can make the bottom of the speedboat.

Bot's Bellyscreen showed Team Umizoomi how to get to the well. First, they had to take a speedboat down the river. Then they had to ride a bulldozer across the farm. Last, they had to take a balloon over the mountain.

"It's time for action!" the team cheered.

Suddenly, the Umi Alarm rang. *"Sizzling Circuits!"* Bot exclaimed. "Brownie the cat is in a well and she can't get out. We have to rescue her."

"I'm giving my bunny, Whispers, some water," said Milli.

"Each of my ants gets one piece of ant food," said Bot, shaking food from a can.

How many ants does Bot have?

It was a busy morning at Umi Headquarters. Team Umizoomi were feeding their pets.

"My pet sea horse, Fin, likes diamond-shaped food," said Geo.

SAVE THE KITTEN

Based on the episode "The Kitty Rescue" by Dustin Ferrer

Illustrated by Bob Ostrom

A Random House PICTUREBACK® Book

Random House 🏠 New York

© 2014 Viacom International Inc. All rights reserved. Published in the United States by Random House Children's Books, a division of Random House, Inc., 1745 Broadway, New York, NY 10019, and in Canada by Random House of Canada Limited, Toronto. Pictureback, Random House, and the Random House colophon are registered trademarks of Random House, Inc. Nickelodeon, Team Umizoomi, and all related titles, logos, and characters are trademarks of Viacom International Inc.
randomhouse.com/kids
ISBN 978-0-385-37520-7
MANUFACTURED IN CHINA
10 9 8 7 6 5 4 3 2